P9-CAO-360

I am an ARO PUBLISHING
TEN WORD BOOK.

My ten words are:

a	eats
dinosaur	and
little	is
cute	big
the	too

Little Dinosaur

10 WORDS

Story and pictures by
BOB REESE

© Copyright 1993 by Aro Publishing Co. All rights reserved, including the right of reproduction in whole or part in any form. Designed and produced by Aro Publishing Co. Printed in the U.S.A. P.O. Box 193 Provo, Utah 84601. Original copyright 1979 by Aro Publishing.

ISBN 0-89868-070-0 — Library Bound
ISBN 0-89868-081-6 — Soft Bound

A dinosaur.

A cute dinosaur.

A little dinosaur.

A cute little

dinosaur.

The cute little dinosaur

eats,

and eats,

and eats,

and eats,

and eats,

and eats,

and eats.

The cute little dinosaur

is big!

The cute big dinosaur

eats and eats.

The big dinosaur

is too BIG!!!